COUNTING ON FRANK

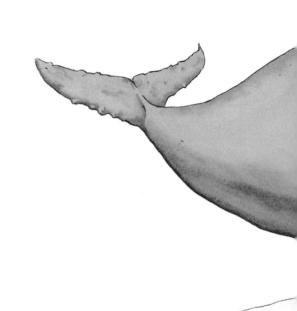

COUNTING *on* FRANK

Written and illustrated by
ROD CLEMENT

Angus&Robertson
An imprint of HarperCollins*Publishers*

in association with
ANNE INGRAM BOOKS

An Angus & Robertson Publication

Angus&Robertson, an imprint of
HarperCollins*Publishers*
25 Ryde Road, Pymble, Sydney, NSW 2073, Australia
31 View Road, Glenfield, Auckland 10, New Zealand

First published in Australia by William Collins Pty Ltd in 1990
in association with Anne Ingram Books
Special edition 1990
Reprinted in 1991 (twice)
This Bluegum paperback edition first published in 1991
Reprinted in 1992, 1994

National Library of Australia
Cataloguing-in-Publication data:

Clement, Rod.
   Counting on Frank.
   ISBN 0 207 17322 2.
   I. Title.
A823.3

Typeset by LetterCraft, St. Leonards, N.S.W.
Printed in Hong Kong

11 10 9 8 7 6
98 97 96 95 94

For Sue

My Dad says, "If you've got a brain, then use it!"
So I do.

I sit down and fill my notebook with facts.
Did you know that the average ballpoint pen
draws a line two thousand and sixty metres
long, before the ink runs out?
My parents consider this fact to be
a bit childish, but I'm sure the
pen company would like to know.

My dog, Frank, is pretty big and takes up
a lot of space.

I calculate that twenty-four Franks could fit
into my bedroom, but sometimes
there isn't even room for one.

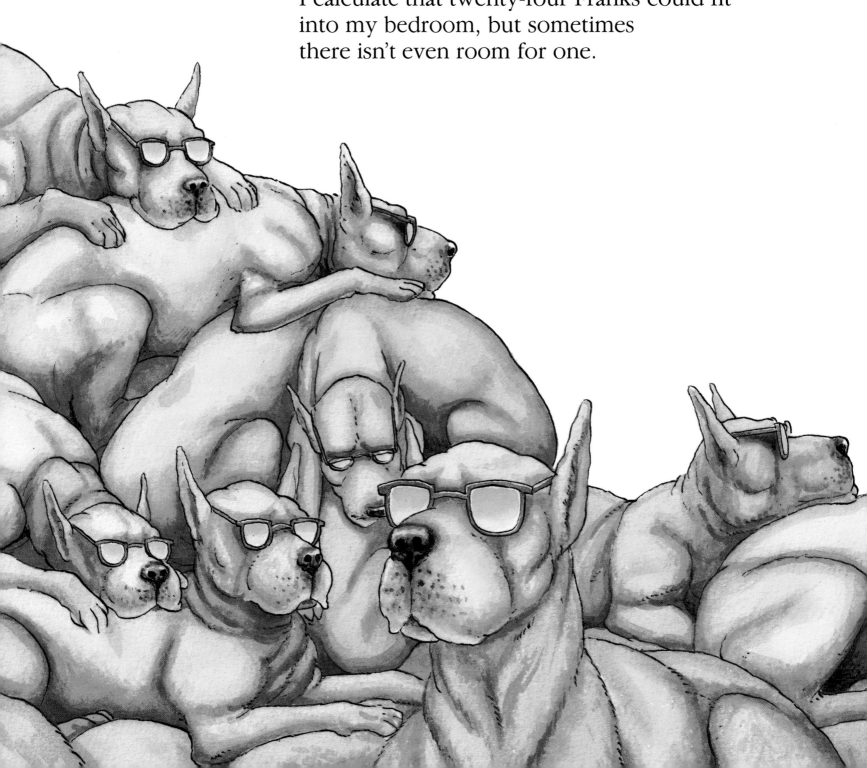

If Frank were a humpback whale, however,
then only ten would fit into our entire house.
I asked Dad about this and he said they would
get in the way of the television.

I calculate that only one Dad would
fit inside our big television,
but only one-tenth of him would fit
in Mum's portable.
Mum said she would prefer the top part
because Dad's feet smell.

We've got a gum tree in our garden.
It grows about two metres every year.

If I had grown at the same speed I'd now be
sixteen metres tall!
I wouldn't mind really, except that
I'd never get clothes to fit.

I don't mind having a bath – it gives me time to think.

For example, I calculate it would take eleven hours and forty-five minutes to fill the entire bathroom with water. That's with both taps running.

It would take slightly less time
to empty, as long as
no one opened the door!

When I get dressed I don't think about fashion or style.
I think about facts.

For instance, it's a fact that if I put on every article of clothing
in my cupboard I would be two point eight metres tall
and one point eight metres wide.
I would also be unable to sit down.

I enjoy dinner, not because of the delicious grill Mum cooks EVERY night, or the thrilling conversation.

It's the peas.

If I had accidentally knocked fifteen peas off my plate every night for the last eight years, they would now be level with the table top.

Maybe, then, Mum would understand that her son does *not* like peas.

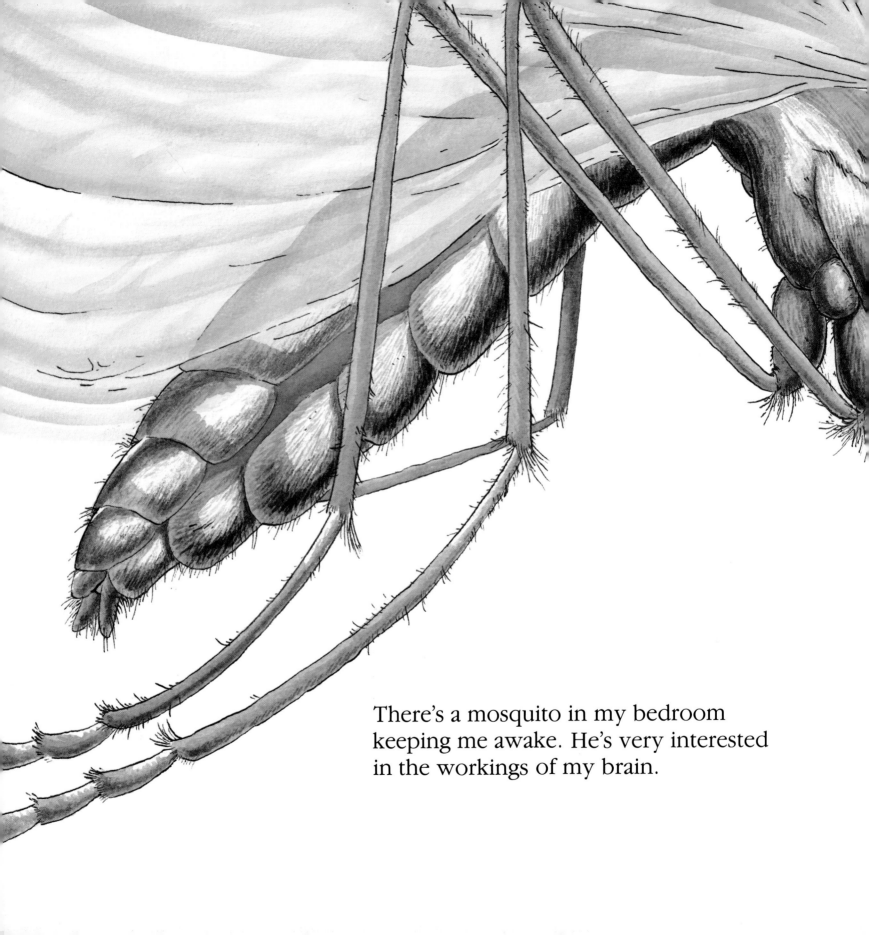

There's a mosquito in my bedroom
keeping me awake. He's very interested
in the workings of my brain.

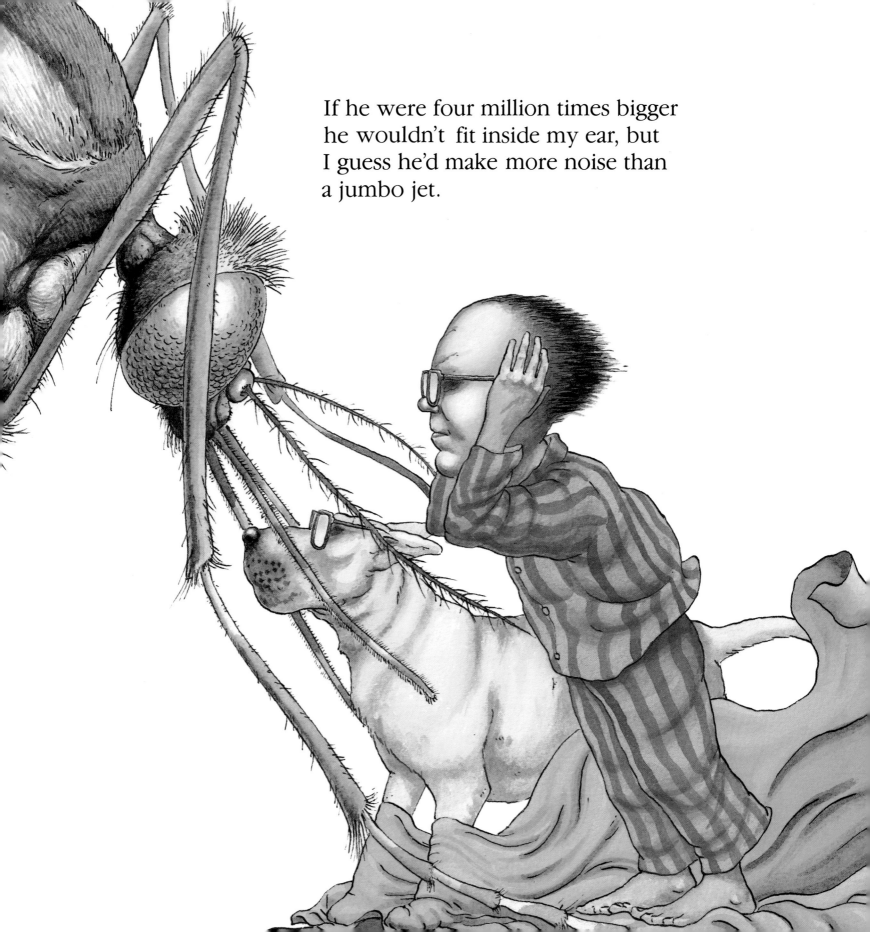

If he were four million times bigger
he wouldn't fit inside my ear, but
I guess he'd make more noise than
a jumbo jet.

At breakfast I have a glass of orange juice and two pieces of toast.

Our old toaster shoots the toast about a metre in the air.

It makes you think – if our toaster were as big as the house, it could endanger low flying aircraft.

Going shopping with Mum is a big event.
She is lucky to have such an intelligent trolley-pusher.

It takes forty-seven cans of dog food to fill one
trolley, but only one to knock over one hundred
and ten!

Because of Frank my knuckles will scrape
along the ground by the time I'm twenty-five!

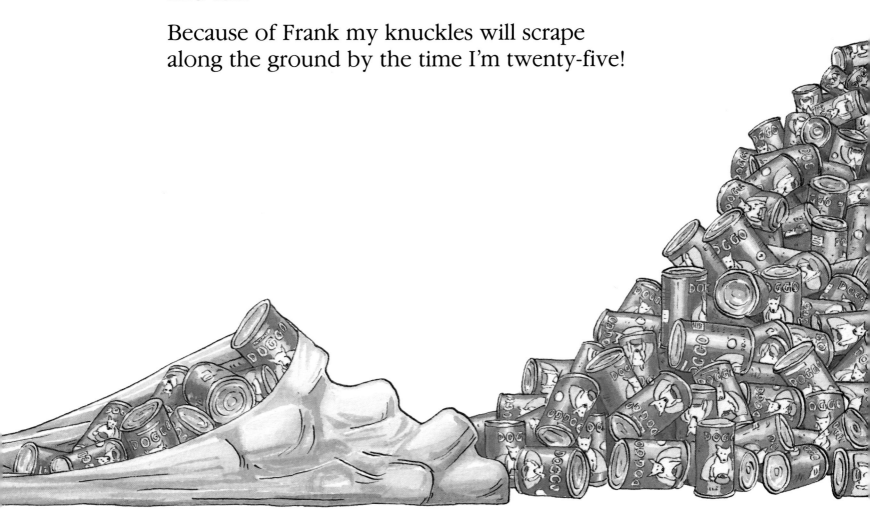

The local club had a competition.
You had to guess how many jelly beans
were in the jar, and the prize was a trip to Hawaii.

They didn't know who they were dealing with.

There are seven hundred and forty-five jelly beans in the average lolly jar – I thought everybody knew that!

As Dad said on the plane to Hawaii,
"If you've got a brain, then use it."